WINNIE'S NEW BROOM

by Tony Bradman   pictures by Jean Baylis

2   Winnie's got a new broom.

3

4 Wally gets on the broom with Winnie.

They fly round the room with a whoosh and a zoom! 5

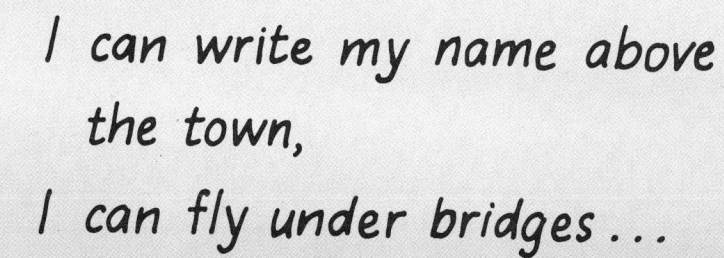

I can write my name above
the town,
I can fly under bridges...

9

Ah! I'm not sure about that.
Let me see now, what does it say here . . .

Look out, Winnie!

It's too late . . .

13